Sarah

Brad

Zach

Mary

Geranium Lady

Joy

Michael

Wumphee

The Geranium Lady Series

The Pepperoni Parade and the Power of Prayer

A Book About Prayer

Barbara Johnson

Illustrations by Victoria Ponikvar Frazier

Tommy
NELSON

Thomas Nelson, Inc.
Nashville

Barbara Johnson's
The Geranium Lady Series
The Pepperoni Parade and the Power of Prayer

Text copyright © 1999 by Barbara Johnson
Illustrations copyright © 1999 by Tommy Nelson™,
a division of Thomas Nelson, Inc.

Concept and Story by A. Clayton

Published in Nashville, Tennessee, by Tommy Nelson™,
a division of Thomas Nelson, Inc. Vice President of Children's Books: Laura Minchew;
Editor: Tama Fortner; Art Director: Karen Phillips.

Scripture quoted from the *International Children's Bible, New Century Version,*
copyright © 1986, 1988 by Word Publishing. Used by permission.

Library of Congress Cataloging-in-Publication Data

Johnson, Barbara (Barbara E.)
  The pepperoni parade and the power of prayer : a book about prayer / Barbara
Johnson ; illustrations by Victoria Ponikvar Frazier.
    p.   cm.—(The Geranium Lady series)
  Summary: When Sarah becomes lost at a large parade, she and her friends learn
the importance of praying for God's help.
  ISBN 0-8499-5950-0
  [1. Lost children—Fiction. 2. Prayer—Fiction. 3. Christian life—Fiction.]
I. Frazier, Victoria Ponikvar, 1966– ill. II. Title. III. Series: Johnson, Barbara (Barbara
E.). Geranium Lady series.
PZ7.J63035Pe   1999
[E]—dc21

                                                                98-51089
                                                                    CIP
                                                                    AC

Printed in the United States of America
99 00 01 02 03 QPH 9 8 7 6 5 4 3 2 1

Letter to Parents

Kids say the funniest things about prayer. Like the little boy who once asked, "If God is really there when I pray, why can't I see Him?" Good question . . . but I always wondered how the boy knew that God wasn't there if his eyes were closed!

Just like the boy, sometimes we need assurance that God really is there when we need Him. But how do we explain a concept like prayer to children and grandchildren? Well . . . that's the purpose of this book—and my entire children's series. You see, I believe that laughter is the sweetest music that ever greeted the human ear. Throughout these pages, my hope is that kids will laugh—and learn some valuable lessons—as they follow the Geranium Lady on her zany adventures.

In this book, kids will learn that God is only a prayer away . . . no matter where they are or how alone they may feel. While I certainly don't have all the answers to life's questions, I know Someone who does. I encourage you to turn all of your questions and problems over to God. Try it today—you'll be much happier with the results!

Celebrating the Power of Prayer,

The Geranium Lady

The Geranium Lady

Drum roll. High kick. Trumpet blast. Crowd cheer. The kids couldn't believe their eyes as the band warmed up in front of them.

As a special treat, the Geranium Lady had brought her six young friends to the town parade.

"Because there are so many people here," said the Geranium Lady,
"I've brought matching purple backpacks to help us all stay together."

As the kids were putting on their backpacks, they heard a loud trumpet blast.

"Let the parade begin," Mayor Piddlesnicker shouted, and a giant cannon shot confetti and balloons high into the air.

First came the band, and then came the big Papa Pepperoni's Pizza Palace balloon. Even the people holding the balloon's ropes were dressed as giant pepperoni!

"That's awesome!" Sarah exclaimed as the huge, pizza-shaped balloon floated by them.

"Doesn't that make you hungry?" Brad asked as he turned to Sarah. But Sarah was no longer there!

Sarah had been so amazed by the pizza balloon that she had walked right up to it to get a closer look. But when she turned around, she couldn't find her friends. *Sarah was lost!*

Sarah walked through the crowd,
hoping to see a familiar face. But she only saw strangers
who were busy clapping and cheering for the parade.

When they discovered that Sarah was lost, the Geranium Lady and the kids all huddled together and began to pray. They asked God to protect Sarah and to help them find her.

"Cheer up, everyone," the Geranium Lady said. "I know a way to find Sarah. I'll be right back. But you must wait here where we last saw Sarah, in case she returns."

The Geranium Lady hurried over to a hot air balloon that was just about to lift off. She asked the owner if she could ride along, hoping to spot Sarah and her purple backpack from above the crowd.

The owner agreed. But as the Geranium Lady was climbing into the basket, her foot accidentally kicked the balloon's rope loose. The balloon started to rise before the owner could jump in!

"Oh, dear!" cried the Geranium Lady. The owner tried to tell her how to land the balloon, but she was already too high in the air to hear him. The Geranium Lady prayed, "God, I was hoping to rescue Sarah. Now I need rescuing, too!"

Sarah was scared. She was beginning to think that she would never find her friends. She prayed, "God, please help me find my way back."

    As the Geranium Lady soared high over the parade, she spotted Sarah. But how could she get the girl's attention? That's when the Geranium Lady suddenly remembered what she had put in each backpack.

Sarah sat down, feeling all alone. "I guess God didn't hear my prayer," she sighed. Just then, she heard a familiar voice—it was the Geranium Lady calling her name!

But when Sarah turned around, the Geranium Lady was nowhere to be seen. "Sarah, it's me," the voice called again. The voice was coming from inside her backpack!

Sarah opened her backpack and found a walkie-talkie. From it the Geranium Lady's voice chirped excitedly, "I put a walkie-talkie in each backpack in case anyone got lost. But I was so busy trying to find you that I forgot all about the walkie-talkies!"

"Where are you?" Sarah asked. The Geranium Lady chuckled,
"I'm . . . um . . . well, look up." Overhead, the balloon was floating higher
and higher.

From her bird's-eye view, the Geranium Lady saw the solution. "Sarah, you need to cross the street. You are only a few feet away from the others—you just can't see them over the parade."

Sarah ran to her friends, and they all thanked God for answering their prayers.

But the Geranium Lady was still stuck in a runaway balloon! Using Sarah's walkie-talkie, the balloon owner was able to guide the Geranium Lady to a safe landing. To celebrate, the parade cannon shot hundreds of geraniums into the air.

Later, the Geranium Lady gathered the kids together. "Prayer is what helped Sarah and me today. God hears all of our prayers. He watches over us from above and guides our lives just like He used me to help guide Sarah back to her friends."

"Even when Sarah felt all alone, she wasn't," the Geranium Lady said. "Just as walkie-talkies let us speak to people we can't see, prayer lets us talk to God—even though we can't see Him."

Sarah smiled. It was good to know that whether you're lost in a crowd or stuck in the clouds, God is only a prayer away.

CALL TO ME IN TIMES OF TROUBLE.
I WILL SAVE YOU, AND YOU WILL HONOR ME.
Psalm 50:15

MAKE YOUR OWN "WALKIE-TALKIE PRAYER BOX"

The real Geranium Lady, Barbara Johnson, has a special prayer starter for you! With a grownup's help, you can make your own giant walkie-talkie that will hold your prayer requests to God. Here's how:

1. Find an empty shoebox. Decorate it with bright, shiny wrapping paper. (Or paint it with tempera paint.) Be sure to wrap the bottom part and the lid of the shoebox separately so you can later lift off the top.

2. Find a sheet of paper the size of the top of your shoebox. On it, draw a walkie-talkie like the one shown on the next page.

3. Color the walkie-talkie. Add sparkly beads and glitter. Carefully cut out the walkie-talkie, and then glue it to the shoebox lid.

4. On a small piece of paper, write your prayer request. Or you could even draw a picture of what you want to talk to God about. Your prayer can be for a friend, a pet, your brother or sister, or your mom or dad. Remember, you can talk to God about anything at all. Say your prayer, then put your requests in your prayer box.

The next time you are ready to talk to God, pull out your prayer requests to see what you need to talk to Him about. You may discover that God has already answered some of your prayers—so be sure to thank Him!